Who Did It?

Written by Jill Eggleton
Illustrated by Jim Storey

Rigby

0757 818846
ISBN

THE SCENE:
POLICE STATION -
**Meeting of Police
Officers.**
The Chief of Police
is working through
the list of tasks
to be undertaken.

We have a problem at Martha's Ice-cream Shop. All her ice cream has disappeared. She had to leave the shop between four and five o'clock on Monday afternoon. She was in a hurry and left the windows open. I have a list of people who visit her shop for ice cream most afternoons.

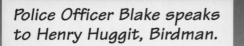

Police Officer Blake speaks to Henry Huggit, Birdman.

Birdman's Diary July

Monday 6

Time	Activity
9:00	Clean bird plops off neighbor's wall.
10:00	Meeting with Jack to discuss leak in the glass roof of the birdhouses.
11:30	Collect new birdbaths from Sam's.
12:00	Meet D. for lunch at Bruno's.
1:30	Salesperson from Birdseed Company.
3:30	Bird rescue - Two baby birds stuck in water pipe on Fenton Street. Catch 2:30 bus. Take scoop, net, and feather box.
7:00	Meeting of Bird Club.

Notes

Monday

I still have not been able to rescue the baby birds that are stuck in the water pipe. I will try again tomorrow. I will need to make a longer handle for my bird rescue scoop. The birds seem to be OK. The kids are feeding them with worms.

I missed my ice cream today. I will have two double scoops tomorrow!

I am sorry I can't be of any help. I wasn't anywhere near Martha's Shop on Monday.

Beekeeper's Diary July

Monday 6

Things to Do Today

MORNING
* Repaint sign on fence.
* Make new bee box.
* Collect bee swarm from Mr. Don's letterbox.

AFTERNOON

1:00 Talk at Briggles School on bee behavior.
Take photographs.

2:30 Check bee swarms at Dale Street to find out why bees are evacuating them.

4:00 Make honey ice cream.

4:20 Phone Martha for an appointment to discuss selling ice cream to her.

4:30 Bee Club meeting.

Notes

A six-year-old kid at Briggles School said he watched a bee doing a tail dance. He said the bee turned in a figure eight 11 times in one minute. He figured out the flower with the food was a mile away! Kids are really clever today!

Martha is interested in buying honey ice cream for her shop. Great!

I did speak on the phone to Martha about the honey ice cream. I didn't visit her at all. I am not much use to your investigation.

NOTES

Monday 6 July

9:00   Meeting with Spy Chief.

10:30   Appointment with Sal at Spy Shop.
Need: new wig – spy shoes – hat.

1:30   Job at Whitlow School – Find out who is
making holes in the books.
Take black glasses and gloves.

3:30   Job at Potters Park – Find out who turns
the park benches upside down.
Wear orange wig and blue coat.

5:00   Training School – Teach "How to Send
and Receive Spy Messages."
Check Billy Napp's homework.

7:00   Job at Fuller's Creek – Find out
who is building dams across
the creek. Wear green
wetsuit and goggles.

10:00   Send code message
to Spy Chief.

July 6

It is hard work training
spies. My students still
can't send secret messages
clearly. The chief is getting
impatient.

I did find out that an old
woman is turning the park
benches upside down so
that the birds can't perch
on them and dirty them.

*Looks like I didn't have time for an ice cream
on Monday. If you need help sorting out this
problem, let me know. It would be a good job.
I could work and eat ice cream at the same
time.*

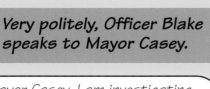

Very politely, Officer Blake speaks to Mayor Casey.

Mayor Casey, I am investigating a burglary at Martha's Ice-cream Shop. I understand that you are a customer. Did you notice anything suspicious on Monday, July 6, in the evening?

I am so busy every day it is impossible for me to remember. I will need to look in my DIGITAL DIARY.

MAYOR

TWEET BIRD SEED

TWEET BIRD SEED

MAYORAL APPOINTMENTS DIARY
JULY 6 — 10

Monday 6

8: 00	Meeting with staff.
10: 00	Speak to reporter from Star.
10: 45	Meeting with Park Manager.
11: 30	**Speak to reporter from Daily.**
12: 30	Open new cheese factory.
1: 00	Lunch with manager.
2: 15	Taxi pick up.
2: 30	**Radio Show:** **Debate - Getting Rid of Alley Cats From City.**
4: 00	Office. Check e-mails.
5: 30	Dinner with visiting mayors.
7: 45	Taxi pick up.
8: 00	**Speak to Bird Club -** **Topic: Free Bird Seed for City Birds.**

MONDAY NOTES

Alley Cat Debate very interesting.
I am not wanting to get rid of the alley cats. They do a good job. They keep the mice away from the streets. Will have a meeting with shop owners to see what they think.

○ QUIT
○ EXIT

As you can see from my appointments, I was very busy on Monday and didn't have time for an ice cream.

11

Reporter's Diary

Week Ending July 12 - Monday, July 6

10:00	Meeting with Mayor Casey
11:00	Pick up photographer
11:30	Interview the Dennys about their new house. Write a report for Tuesday's paper
12:15	Opening of cheese factory
2:00	Football Game at Pine Park – Captain of Bumbies, Marc Snicker
5:30	Visiting mayors' dinner

Monday Notes

Mayor Casey is worried about alley cat problem. He didn't feel they were causing real problems. Have done an excellent job in keeping mice away. Shopkeepers feel they are keeping customers away.

Cheese factory will provide jobs for 60 people.

Bumbies played Roncos. Bumbies won 32-30. Marc Snicker quote: "It was a tough game. Roncos have excellent runners. It was just as well the bell rang. Bumbies were dropping like flies."

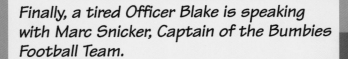

Monday July 6

7: 30   Training — work on tackling
9: 00   Gym — weightlifting
10: 00 Meeting with coach to plan tactics for
        game against Roncos.
12: 00 Lunch with Sally
1: 00   Meeting with team — work out plan for game.
2: 00   Play Roncos — Pine Park
6: 00   Dinner — Brett's Club.

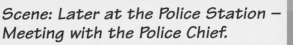

Can I have a report on the investigation at Martha's Ice-cream Shop?

I spoke to all the people who visit Martha's Ice-cream Shop. Marc Snicker was the only person who went to the shop on Monday but it was closed. He saw a bunch of alley cats cleaning their whiskers.

I looked in Martha's shop for clues. I found cat footprints. They went over the window ledge, over the floor, and up the sides of the ice-cream vats.

RASPBERRY

BANANA

I traced another group going back, but this group were ice-cream prints.

I noticed marks at the bottom and sides of the ice-cream vats that were very like the marks a cat's tongue makes when it licks.

I saw cat fur on the window ledge. I think some alley cats entered through the open windows and licked up every drop of Martha's ice cream.

No wonder those Alley Cats have been hanging around Martha's shop. I guess we can close the investigation.

Formal Diary

A formal diary keeps a record of things to do, events to come, and appointments to keep.

How to Keep a Formal Diary

STEP 1 Decide on how long you want to keep the diary for – one day, one week, one month, one year ...

STEP 2 Make a table of the things you want to keep in the diary.

July 6		
THINGS TO DO	APPOINTMENTS	THINGS TO GET
Rescue birds	D. lunch	Bird bath
Clean cages	Meeting Bird Club	Scoop
	Meeting Jack	Net
	Bird Seed Salesperson	Feather box

STEP 3   Look at your table. Can you add a time to the entries?

9:00am	Clean cages
1:30pm	Meet salesperson from seed company

STEP 4   Now write up your diary. If your entries have a time, put them in the correct sequence.

STEP 5   Check your diary.

Is there anything you have forgotten?

Have you got enough time to do the things you have listed?

▬▬ Guide Notes

Title: Who Did It?
Stage: Fluency (3)

Text Form: Formal Diary
Approach: Guided Reading
Processes: Thinking Critically, Exploring Language, Processing Information
Written and Visual Focus: Formal Diaries

THINKING CRITICALLY
(sample questions)
- Why do you think it is important for some people to keep a formal diary like the ones shown in the book?
- What things are the same about all the diaries?
- What is different about the mayor's diary compared to the reporter's diary?
- Why do you think some of the diaries have a place for notes?

EXPLORING LANGUAGE

Terminology
Spread, author, illustrator, credits, imprint information, ISBN number

Vocabulary
Clarify: investigation, suspicious, evacuating, appointment, impatient, digital, tactics
Adjectives: *tough* game, *excellent* runners
Homonyms: two/two, bee/be, tail/tale, buy/by, blue/blew
Antonyms: impatient/patient, closed/opened, outside/inside, impossible/possible
Synonyms: evacuate/empty, clever/intelligent, appointment/meeting
Abbreviation: p.m. (post meridiem)
Simile: dropping *like flies*

Print Conventions
Dash, colon, apostrophe – possessive (Martha's ice-cream shop, mayors' dinner, cat's tongue, neighbor's wall)